For all my lovely Skyros students – J.D.

For Charlie and Monty Morton – P.D.

First published in Great Britain and in the USA in 2016 by
Otter-Barry Books, Little Orchard, Burley Gate, Hereford, HR1 3QS
www.otterbarrybooks.com

A catalogue record for this book is available
from the British Library.

ISBN 978-1-91095-907-7

Illustrated with mixed media
Set in Malandra GD

Printed in China

1 3 5 7 9 8 6 4 2

I Will not Wear Pink

Story by Joyce Dunbar

Pictures by Polly Dunbar

Otter-Barry BOOKS

What's this?
An invitation?

Dear Plunkett,

Please come to my party.

Theme: Pink. Dream.

Fancy. Frills. Thrills.

Yours oinky,

Priscilla

Pink?
Frills?
Me?

Not likely.

No!

Never. . . .

Not
for
nothing
I'm called
Plunkett the plonker,
Plunkett the oinker.
The hooter, the honker.
The toff who shows off,
stands out in a crowd.

You can poke me
or stroke me,
you can grin,
you can wink.

But nothing
and no one
will
make
me
wear
PINK.

You may think that in pink
I look such a corker,
I look cooler than cool,
hotter than hotter.
I *know* it's a party
with buns and balloons,
but I don't want to preen,
I don't want to prance.

I don't want to **hip hop**

in a plinky plonk dance.

Party

For pink is so phooey,
so daffy, so naff,
me dressed in pink
would make a horse laugh.

I'll kick up a fuss,
I'll make a big stink.
But I will not,
just will not,
I will not wear pink.

Cotton candy is dandy,
the pinkest of pinks.

Roses,
cold noses,
flamingoes,
some toes.

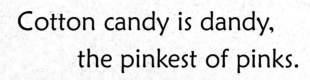

Ballerinas
in tutus –
any pink goes.

In all shades of green, or orange, or yellow,
or all inbetween, I'd look a fine fellow.
I'll wear blue, I'll wear purple,
I'll wear black, I'll wear red.
But in pink,
popsy pink

I WON'T be seen dead.
Dressed up in pink,
no one would see me, no one would stare,
for pink upon pink will look like thin air.
Quite pimply and simply,
they won't
see
I'm there!

FOR. . .

there is one sort of pink
so divine, so sublime,
and the best of it is
that it's already mine, from the tip of my tail

pink is the shade of the skin that I'm in.

to the snoot of my snout,

Pink's where I end and where I begin.

'Cos pink's what I be,
what I is, what I am.
And pink I'll remain
as ham
or as spam.

Pink, piggy pink,
  as you can see,
    is the all over, every bit,
color of me.

So come, dear Priscilla,
you poppet, you thriller,
you're my pooch, come let's smooch.
Let's kiss and canoodle,

let's party and pootle,
   let's tipple and tootle.
      At a junket with Plunkett, my sort of gig,
         you need nothing to wear...

... just come

as a pig!

Come one, come all,
let's have a ball.
Strip off your gear,
take off your clobber,

come wallow with me,
come squish and come slobber.
One sniff of the pong, one whiff of the sty,
then you'll burst into song.
You'll laugh and you'll cry...

Mud, muddy mud,
Blobby brown mud,

Mud is so beautiful,
Mud is so good.

YOU

may do as you please,
you may prink, you may tease.
But ME, as for me,
I'll be true to the hue
that nature intended,
the plunkiest pink,
perfectly blended.

But I will not,
just will not. . .

I
will
not
wear
PINK!